TRAIN TO SOMEWHERE

by Eve Bunting • Illustrated by Ronald Himler

Clarion Books · New York

<u>DEDICATIONS</u>

To Marjorie Naughton—E. B.
For Gloria—R. H.

<u>ACKNOWLEDGMENTS</u>

The author wishes to thank Sandi Burk and Phyllis Muir for their interest and support
in the writing of this book; also Mary Ellen Johnson of the Orphan Train Riders Research Center
and Toni Weiler, who traveled West herself on an Orphan Train when she was two years old.

Clarion Books
a Houghton Mifflin Company imprint
215 Park Avenue South, New York, NY 10003
Text copyright © 1996 by Eve Bunting
Illustrations copyright © 1996 by Ronald Himler

Illustrations executed in watercolor and gouache on Arches 140-lb. hot-press watercolor paper.
Text is 14/18-point Garamond.

Manufactured in China

Library of Congress Cataloging-in-Publication Data

Bunting, Eve, 1928–
Train to Somewhere / Eve Bunting ; illustrated by Ronald Himler
p.   cm.
Summary: In the late 1800s, Marianne travels westward on the Orphan Train in hopes of being placed with a caring family.
ISBN 0-395-71325-0   PA ISBN 0-618-04031-5
[1. Orphans—Fiction. 2. Orphan trains—Fiction.] I. Himler, Ronald, ill. II. Title.
PZ7.B91527Tq   1996
[Fic]—dc20   95-6787
CIP
AC

SCP 20 19 18 17

INTRODUCTION

From the mid-1850s till the late 1920s, an estimated 100,000 homeless children were sent by train from New York City to small towns and farms in the Midwest. Charles Loring Brace of the Children's Aid Society hoped to place them with caring families.

Some of the children did well. Some did not. Some exchanged one kind of misery for another. Some found security and even love.

This is the story of fourteen orphan children, going West, dreaming of a better life. The Orphan Train itself is real; the route it takes and the place names are fictional. The town of Somewhere exists only on the map of the author's imagination.

"This is our train, Marianne," Miss Randolph says, and Nora clutches at my hand.

A conductor comes along the platform. "Are these the orphans, ma'am?" he asks.

Miss Randolph stands very straight. "Fourteen of them."

"We put on a special coach for you at the back," the conductor says.

The big boys carry the trunks and we take the rest of the bundles. Miss Randolph brings the emergency bag. This past week I watched her pack it with washcloths, medicine, and larkspur in case there are some stowaway fleas. None of us from St. Christopher's has any, of course. But those from the other homes and from the streets might.

"Going for a placing-out, are you?" the conductor asks Nora. "My, you look nice!"

"Thank you," Nora says. She's only five, but at St. Christopher's they teach us manners early.

"Good luck!" he says to me. "I hear there are still a lot of people in the New West wanting children to adopt."

"Yes, indeed," Miss Randolph says.

"We're not seeing as many going this year as last, though," the conductor adds. "1877 was a peak year for orphans."

We go aboard.

The train seats are hard. I let Nora sit by the window. We can see ourselves reflected in its dirty glass. She's wearing her new blue coat with the shiny buttons. Her hair twirls in bright ringlets under her bonnet. I can see my own long, thin face. I'm not pretty. I know Nora will be one of the first ones taken.

"Marianne?" She's got my hand again. "Will they believe we're sisters? We don't look a bit alike. I couldn't bear it if they split us up. Let's not go if . . ."

"Shh!" I whisper.

But Miss Randolph has heard. "What's this?" she asks. "It won't work pretending to be sisters." Her voice softens. "Girls, listen. Most of the people will only want one child. Don't spoil it for each other."

It's all right, I tell myself. I slide my fingers into my pocket and touch the softness of the feather. *She'll be there. She'll want me.*

The train's moving. We're gliding fast and smooth past freight yards, past tenements with washing strung on lines, past warehouses. Then we're in the country and there are trees, trees with apples hanging on them. I knew this was the way apples grew but I'd never seen such a thing before.

Miss Randolph has me and another big girl, Jean, hold up a blanket to separate the boys from the girls. She opens one of the trunks and gives us our old clothes. We're to change.

"We don't want you looking messy at the first stop," she says.

She holds the blanket for Jean and me. We fold our new clothes and put them back into the trunks.

After a while we make sandwiches from the loaves and fillings Miss Randolph has brought and we have thick milk out of a can. When it gets dark we sleep, sitting up, leaning against one another.

The wheels mumble all night long.

Clickety-clack, clickety-clee,
I'm coming, Mama. Wait for me.

At Chicago we carry everything out and change trains. Then we're on our way again.

Days and nights have passed since we left New York. Now there's nothing to see outside but grass everywhere, rolling into the distance.

"The Great Plains," Miss Randolph tells us. She shows us in the atlas she's brought. Miss Randolph has made this trip with other orphans, other times. She says that now we should change back into our new clothes.

Not long after that we hear the call: "Porterville, Illinois!" This is our first stop. The town of Somewhere, Iowa, will be our last.

A crowd is waiting on the little platform.

"Cor blimey!" Zachary Cummings breathes when he sees so many people. Zachary came to New York on a boat from Liverpool, England, with his father, and then his father left him. Zachary has a funny way of saying things.

He's the first one out behind Miss Randolph.

There's a gentleman with a big box camera on legs. There are horses and wagons and dogs barking. I can see right away that my mother isn't here. She probably went farther west, farther than this.

A man leads us to the city hall with everyone following, like a parade.

"Smile and look pleasant," Miss Randolph whispers.

We sit on chairs on a stage and the people from the town look us over. They feel the boys' muscles through their coats. They say things like: "This here's a good one." And, "He'll be useful come harvest."

Zachary is taken right away along with two other big boys.

"Cheerio, mates," he calls to us.

Mavis Perkins is chosen by a little, scrawny woman. Mavis is tall and a bit heavy. She has a round face and the sweetest dimples.

"Dorothea!" the little woman calls out to another woman, just as scrawny. "Look at the one I got. She'll be a big help to me in the house. You should get one for your place."

"Mavis is a dear girl," Miss Randolph says as she signs the agreement papers. "Be good to her." She has her lips pressed tightly together. "There'll be an agent coming round to make sure the children are all right."

"So you think I won't treat her well, Missus? Is that what you're saying?" The woman glares at Miss Randolph. "Do you want me to give her back?"

Miss Randolph doesn't say anything. She hands over the papers, and the scrawny woman leads Mavis away.

A man and a woman stop in front of us.

My knees start trembling.

The woman has a soft fur muff. The man's carrying a cane with a gold head.

"Oh, Herbert. How sweet that little girl is!" The woman smiles at Nora. "Can we take her, Herbert? Can we?"

"This is my sister," Nora whispers, tugging at my hand. "Please, please, if you take me can you take her, too?"

"Oh, dear!" The woman looks at Miss Randolph. "We couldn't possibly. We only want one little girl."

"Of course. And they're not sisters, just friends," Miss Randolph says quickly. "Now, stand up, Nora. You help her, Marianne."

I have to pry Nora's fingers from mine.

The woman bends down. "Do you know what's waiting for you in our carriage? A puppy, just for you."

"I don't want a puppy. I want Marianne," Nora cries.

Miss Randolph and the couple sign the agreement papers, and then they take her.

Nora's still crying and looking back.

I'm sniffling, too.

But it's better if I'm not taken. I have to stay free for my mother. She told me she'd come for me. She kneeled in front of me on the steps of St. Christopher's the day she left me there. She was working in Gerrison's chicken factory at the time, and there was a white feather caught in her hair.

I lifted it off and held it against my cheek.

"I'm going West to make a new life for us," she said. "Then I'll come for you."

"When, Mama? When?" The feather stuck against the tears that ran down my face.

"Before Christmas," she said.

I've waited through so many Christmases.

But now I'm going West, too.

Nine of us are left to get back on the train. Miss Randolph says we're to keep on our good clothes. We'll be getting off again soon.

At Kilburn we are walked to a hardware store to stand in line.

"I expect they took all the biggest boys in Porterville," one man says. "But still . . ."

Eddie Hartz, who is only seven, is taken. There's a boy who can stand on his hands and pretend to pull buttons out of people's ears. He makes the crowd laugh and he gets taken, too.

As soon as the train has loaded on wood and fresh water, the rest of us get back aboard.

Miss Randolph wipes her eyes. "Anything's better than being on the streets of New York," she says. "A lot of you will do fine."

"We weren't on the streets," Susan Ayers says. Susan's only five, same as Nora, but she's sassy and not sweet. She was at St. Christopher's, too.

"We couldn't keep all of you forever." Miss Randolph blows her nose on her white handkerchief. "We have to make room. There are other orphans in need."

Susan makes a face.

The next station is Glover. The crowd is smaller. My mother isn't here, either. Where is she? She must know I might be on this train. The story was in all the newspapers, Miss Randolph said. "Orphans from St. Christopher's among those riding the rails." "Children in need of homes." The papers listed every stop. I was sure my mother would be at one of them.

Wait, Mama, wait! I'm coming! Night after night at St. Christopher's I'd send my thoughts to her across the darkness and the distance. *You don't even have to come get me, Mama. I'm coming to you.* But where is she?

At Glover they line us up along the railway track.

Susan's pouting and whining. She says her new boots hurt her feet.

There's a nice-looking man and woman at the front of the crowd.

Susan stops pouting. She smiles and holds up her arms.

"Mama! Papa!" she begs.

The woman clutches at her heart. "James! She's calling out to us."

The man scoops Susan into his arms. "We'll take her," he says.

"Can I have a puppy?" Susan asks.

The man smiles. "I'll just bet you can, honey."

A boy who has his eyeglasses tied on with string is taken, too, and two other boys.

"There's not much left to pick from," a woman says in a bad-tempered way. "Next time we'll have to ride in as far as Porterville."

I have a terrible hurt inside of me. My mother didn't want me. It looks like nobody wants me. It's not that I'm hoping to be placed, because my mother could be at the very next stop. But what if she isn't?

The three of us who are left get back on the train with Miss Randolph. She gives us gingersnaps and milk from the can she got in Glover. The milk is sweet.

"We can't be down in the dumps, children," she says. "Let's sing." She begins, "Jesus loves me," but nobody joins in. She sings alone through three verses.

We're such a long way from Nora. I wonder if her puppy has a name. If somebody takes me, I'll ask if we can go visit her. "She's like my sister," I'll say.

"Memorial," the conductor calls. There are four people waiting at the station. None of them is my mother. I stumble out with the girl named Amy and the one named Dorothy. We sneak glances at one another. We're wondering which one of us looks best. They're not pretty, either. The taste of the sweet milk is still in my throat and it's making me sick.

One couple takes both Amy and Dorothy. "Two for the price of one," the man jokes, though of course there is no price.

"Marianne is very good with children," Miss Randolph tells the other couple. There's a sort of begging in her voice as she clutches the last agreement form, the one for me.

"My missus looks after our little one," the man grumps.

"We just came to look," the woman says. "But . . ." She takes an apple from her bag and gives it to me. "Have this, child."

"Thank you." I bend my head over the apple. It is blurry through my tears.

The train whistle's blowing.

Miss Randolph and I get on. There's only one stop left, I know. One.

Miss Randolph says I should eat my apple. She says she has a washcloth in case my hands get sticky. I say I don't want to eat anything just yet.

We look out the window, not talking, not singing. Miss Randolph has me take off my hat and she brushes my hair.

"There's a nice hotel farther down the line," she says. "If there's nobody at this next stop, why, we'll just go on. I'll be glad of the company. And on the journey back."

"Somewhere," the conductor calls. It's such a strange name. As if it thinks itself important. As if it's a place surrounded by nowhere.

I put my hat back on. My hands are shaking.

Outside there's a couple waiting by a wagon. The woman is small and round as a dumpling. She's wearing a heavy black dress and a man's droopy black hat. She is not my mother.

"Are you ready, Marianne?" Miss Randolph asks softly.

I pull myself back into the corner of the seat. "No," I whisper. "No."

Miss Randolph holds my hand as we get down from the train.

The man is tall and stooped. He takes off his hat.

The woman doesn't take hers off.

I think they're both pretty old. The woman's holding a wooden toy locomotive.

"Are you . . . ?" the man asks Miss Randolph.

"Yes." Miss Randolph nudges me forward. "This is Marianne."

"Is she all . . ." The woman stops. I know she was going to say: "Is she all that's left?" But she doesn't. She looks at me closely and I see a change in her face. A softness. I'd thought my mother would look at me like that.

Somehow this woman understands about me, how it felt that nobody wanted me, even though I was waiting inside myself for my mother to come. Somehow she understands the hurt.

"I'm Tillie Book," she tells Miss Randolph. "This here's my husband, Roscoe." She holds the toy locomotive out to me. "We brought you this."

"I'm not what you wanted, am I?" I say. "You wanted a boy." The locomotive has red painted wheels and a blue smokestack.

"I won't lie to you. We did want a boy," Mrs. Book says.

"But we like girls fine," Mr. Book adds.

Mrs. Book squints at me. "I expect we're not what you wanted, either. Roscoe and I, we found each other late in life. I always thought I'd catch myself somebody a mite more handsome." She pats Mr. Book's hand and they smile at each other, and I can tell they like each other a lot. "Sometimes what you get turns out to be better than what you wanted in the first place," Mrs. Book says.

"Yes." There's a sort of crumbling inside of me. My mother's not in Somewhere. She's not waiting here or anywhere. "I . . ." I reach in my pocket and bring out the feather. It was white when I took it from my mother's hair; now it's yellow. I smooth it with my fingers. "I brought you this."

"Why, thank you." Mrs. Book sticks the feather in the band of her droopy hat. It's funny the way it nestles there, as if it belongs, as if it has found its place at last.

Mr. Book takes the agreement papers, looks at them, then at me. "Will you come with us?"

"Yes," I whisper.

Miss Randolph leans forward and kisses my cheek.
"Are you ready now, Marianne?" she asks.
"I'm ready."